To Katja
Britta

LITTLE TIGER KIDS

An imprint of Little Tiger Group

1 The Coda Centre, 189 Munster Road, London SW6 6AW

www.littletiger.co.uk • First published in Great Britain 2016

Text by Patricia Hegarty

Text copyright © 2016 Little Tiger Press

Illustrations copyright © Britta Teckentrup 2016

All rights reserved • ISBN: 978-1-84869-316-6

Printed in China •LTK/1800/0517/0517

10 9 8 7 6 5 4 3 2

BEE

Illustrated by Britta Teckentrup

Dawn is breaking on a brand new day
And in the meadow, poppies sway.

ped black and gold;
is about to unfold.

In the treetops, b
The little bee b

here and there,
ming fills the air.

Back and forth, to

The bee knows exactl

...wers of every hue,

...pecial job to do.

Gathering nectar as she goes,
From every foxglove, every rose.
Dusty with pollen, the little bee
Buzzes, buzzes, busily.

Bee travels on from bloom to bloom,
Drawn in by their sweet perfume.

Harvesting flowers one by one;
Her compass is the midday sun.

Among the orchard's apple trees,
Blossom quivers in the breeze.

Carrying pollen from place to place,
Bee always leaves a tiny trace.

Flowers as far as the eye can see –
Too many flowers for just one bee.

All of a sudden, Bee is gone –
She has a message to pass on.

Back at the hive, Bee spreads the news,
There's work to be done – no time to lose...

Listen for their gentle humming –
The word is out; the bees are coming!

Buzzing over the dense hedgerows,
Past the pond, where wild thyme grows.

Through the orchard's sweet-smelling scent,
The bees travel on with calm intent.

As lilies glow orange in the sun,
The bees must finish what they've begun.

Stopping at every flower they find,
Leaving the gift of pollen behind.

The bees pass over a woodland stream,
Droplets sparkle and pebbles gleam.

Water trickles, bubbles and weaves,
A weeping willow trails its leaves.

As the bees fly on through buds and burrs,
A tiny miracle occurs.

For every plant and flower you see
Was given life by one small bee.